# Crazy Creature
# Capers

Written by
# Hannah Reidy

Illustrated by
# Clare Mackie

The
crazy
creatures
put on
their
skates...

and
whizz
**down**
the
road.

To the party.

They
swoosh
**under**
the
crazy
bridge…

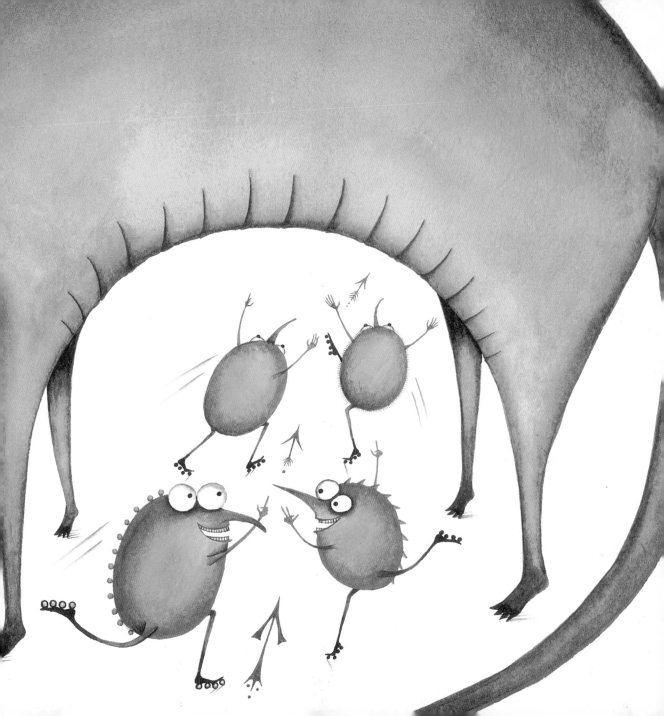

and
glide
between
the
crazy
trees.

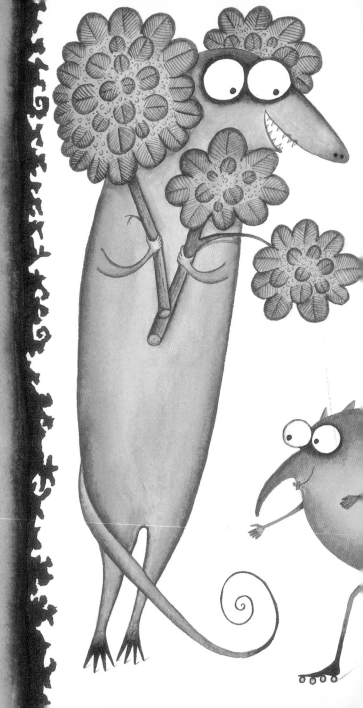

They
puff
and puff
and puff
**UP** the
crazy
hill...

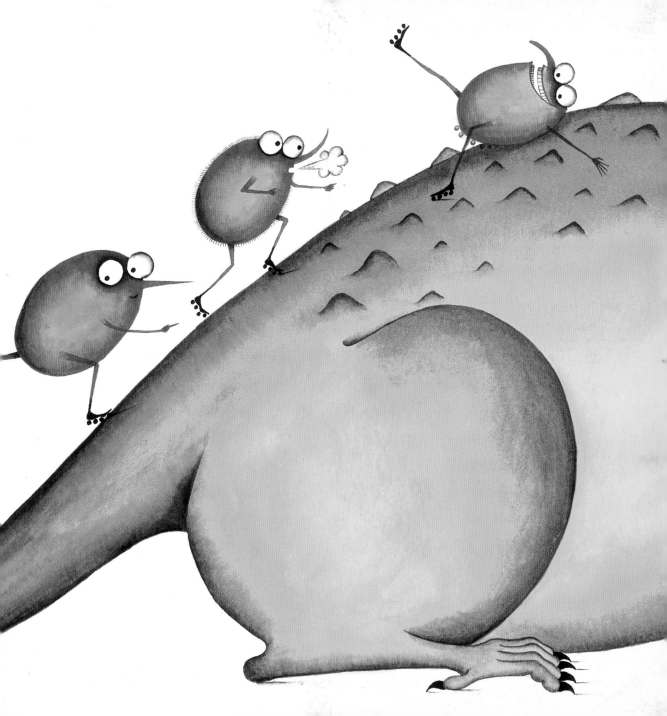

and
tumble
**over**
the
knobbly
bumps.

They
whoosh
**through**
the
crazy
tunnel...

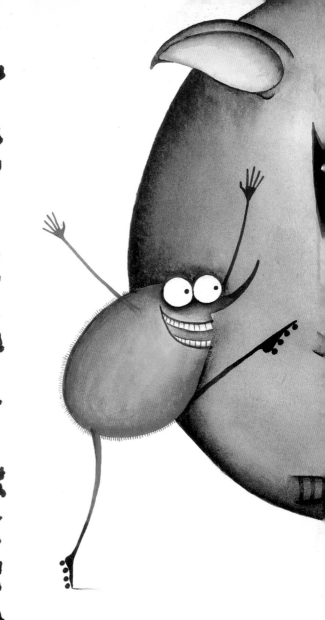

# and arrive **at** the crazy party!